THE LAST ONE IS A ROTTEN EGG

by Tina Gagliardi   illustrated by Patrick Girouard

visit us at www.abdopublishing.com

Printed in the United States.

Text by Tina Gagliardi
Illustrations by Patrick Girouard
Edited by Nadia Higgins and Jill Sherman
Interior layout and design by Nicole Brecke
Cover design by Nicole Brecke

Library of Congress Cataloging-in-Publication Data

Gagliardi, Tina.
  The last one is a rotten egg / by Tina Gagliardi ; illustrated by Patrick Girouard.
     p. cm. — (Carly's dragon days)
  ISBN 978-1-60270-598-2
  [1. Dragons—Fiction.] I. Girouard, Patrick, ill. II. Title.
  PZ7.G1242Las 2009
  [E]—dc22
                              2008035937

Carly was the youngest of 843 brothers and sisters. Even though 23 of her siblings still lived at home, she had her own room. Well, except for Gretchen, her imaginary human friend, and Salvador, the 100-year-old egg in the corner.

Salvador was one of Carly's brothers, but he had not hatched.

Salvador hadn't always slept in Carly's room. He used to stay with other family members, too. Then the egg grew to be five feet tall and three feet wide!

Carly's brothers and sisters complained that Salvador took up too much space. Late at night, whoever had been stuck with the egg would roll Salvador into someone else's room. It was no easy task!

Carly's siblings were afraid of Salvador because of an old dragon tale. The legend said that if a 100-year-old egg hatched, the dragon inside would be horribly mean.

No other family had ever had such an old dragon egg. So Carly's family had become famous. Every spring the whole town would gather to see if the egg would finally hatch.

On the morning the egg appeared in Carly's room, Gretchen asked, "What's this?"

Carly explained Salvador's problem to Gretchen.

"Do you think we should do anything with the egg?" Gretchen asked.

Carly looked at the egg and shrugged. "No, I don't think I'll mind sharing my room with Salvador."

It bothered Carly that everyone was afraid of Salvador. No one had even had a chance to get to know him.

That night, Carly covered Salvador with a blanket. She whispered, "I don't think you take up too much space, Sal. You can stay here for as long as you want."

*C*rack . . . *Crack* . . . *Crackle* . . . At dawn, Carly awoke to a strange noise. She looked at the egg and saw a large crack in Salvador's shell.

"Salvador is breaking loose!" she yelled.

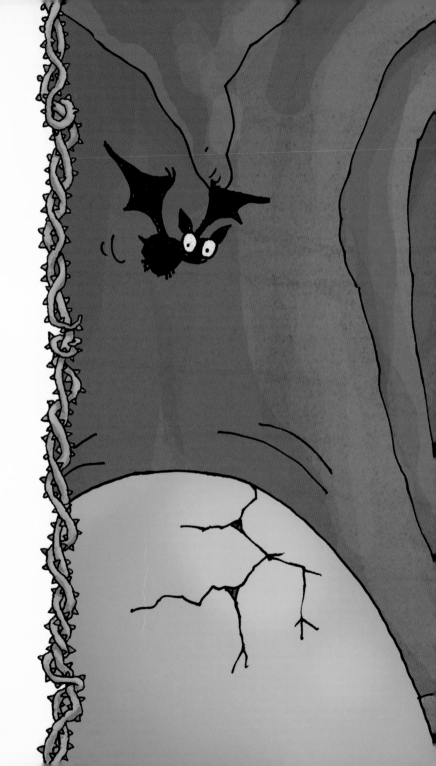

All 23 of Carly's brothers and sisters ran into her room. They stood back and watched as the egg shook wildly. Salvador was breaking free!

Tiny pieces of shell flew everywhere. They covered the cave floor. At last, Salvador made his way out of his egg.

Usually, newly hatched dragons were greeted cheerfully by their brothers and sisters. Carly's siblings just stared at Salvador. No one said a word.

Salvador looked around expectantly. After a minute, an angry look came over his face. He leaped forward and hissed so loudly that everyone in the room jumped back.

They all began to shout, "The legend was right. He's a no-good, rotten egg!"

Salvador ran out of the room. Booms, crashes, and even sizzles could be heard far below. Carly sniffed. Was that a burning smell?

Carly chased after Salvador. She had to find him before he destroyed the whole cave!

Carly heard crashing coming from the kitchen. She ran to see what was going on. Carly searched every corner of the room, but Salvador had vanished.

What a mess! Carly thought. She had to stop Salvador right away!

"Salvador!" Carly called, but no one answered. The cave had grown completely quiet.

Carly walked through every tunnel in the cave, but there was no sign of Salvador.

Finally, Carly gave up and went back to her room. To her surprise, there was Salvador! Her little brother was crying.

"Are you okay?" Carly asked.

"Everyone is afraid of me," Salvador sobbed. "I have heard them all say that I was going to be a mean dragon. I thought once they met me they would stop being afraid, but they still are."

"Maybe they just need time to get to know you," Carly said.

Just then, Carly heard a noise. She looked up to find her brothers and sisters standing outside.

Carly and Salvador's brother Robert stepped forward. "We're sorry, Salvador," he said.

Then, everyone came inside to meet Salvador. For the first time ever, the baby dragon smiled. He cheerfully met all his brothers and sisters, just like a newly hatched dragon should!

What do you recall from Carly's Dragon Days?

1. How long has Salvador been inside his egg?

2. What do Carly's brothers and sisters do with Salvador's egg at night?

3. What do Carly's brothers and sisters think will happen when Salvador hatches?

4. Why does Salvador make a mess of the cave?

5. Who makes Salvador feel better?

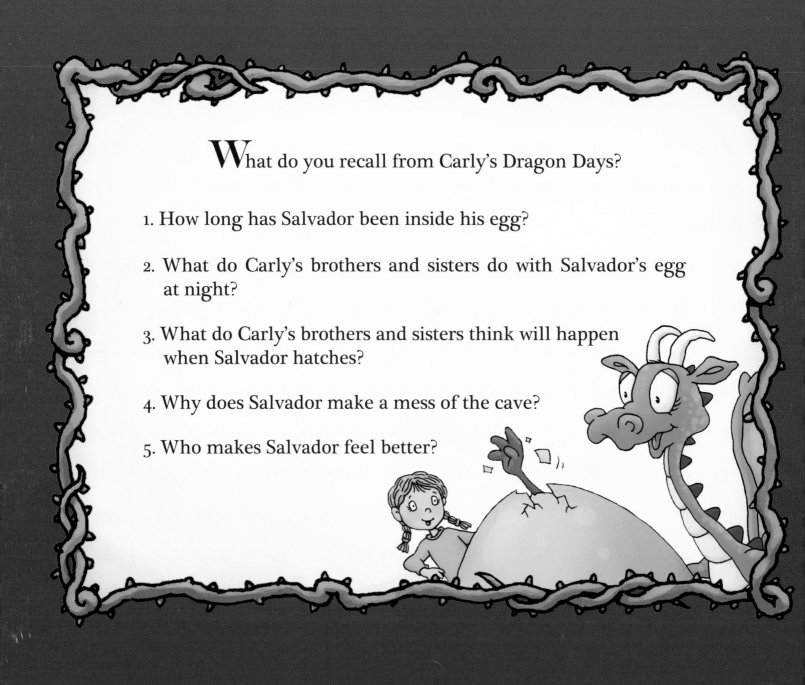